Who's New at the Zoo?

written by Lori C. Froeb
illustrated by Pixel Mouse House

Reader's Digest
Children's Books®

New York, New York • Montréal, Québec • Bath, United Kingdom

Who is new at the zoo? Eddie and his friends want to find out! Zookeeper Mack greets them at the zoo entrance. Today is the day that all the baby animals come out to meet everyone for the first time. "Who wants to meet the baby animals?" he asks.

"We do!" the friends shout.

"Are there any lion cubs?" asks Sonya Lee. "They are my favorite!"

"I'm afraid that we haven't seen any lion cubs this year," answers Zookeeper Mack. "But we have lots of other adorable babies. Let's find them."

First, the group finds a wrinkly gray baby that is as big as Zookeeper Mack.

"It's an elephant calf," says Eddie. "His trunk tickles!"

"Welcome, baby elephant," says Sarah Lynn. "You are so big already!"

"Elephants are the biggest land animals," says Zookeeper Mack. "This baby weighs as much as a grown-up human."

"They must eat a lot," says Michael.

"They sure do," says Mack, "and their long trunks come in handy for picking food off the ground!"

What's brown and white and cute all over? It's a zebra foal! And she is the next baby the friends find.

"I thought zebras had black stripes," says Sonya Lee. "Why does this foal have brown stripes?"

"That's a great question," says Mack. "Zebra babies are born with brown stripes to help them hide in the brown grass of the savannah where they live."

"That's neat," says Sonya Lee. "She runs really fast for a baby."

"She's had a lot of practice," says Mack. "Zebra foals can run very soon after being born."

"Let's meet some roly poly babies that *are* black and white," says Mack. "These are our panda bears!"

"Wow!" says Michael. "They sit while eating just like people do!"

"It looks like they are eating branches," says Maggie.

"Yes, pandas eat a plant called bamboo," says Mack. "Bamboo is a plant that grows in China where they live."

"Hey! Look up there," shouts Eddie, pointing to a tree's branches. "There is a koala giving her baby a piggyback ride!"

"That's right, Eddie," Mack says, laughing. "A baby koala is called a joey and that is how the mother keeps her baby close."

"Her arms must be strong to climb like that," adds Sarah Lynn.

"Yes, they are," answers Mack. "When the joey is very small, it stays in a special pouch on its mother's tummy—just like a kangaroo!"

Freddie hops over to his favorite habitat—the reptile house—
and the friends follow. "Wow!" squeals Michael. "Baby snakes!"
   "And I see baby tortoises over there," Eddie says, excitedly.
"They are so little."

Zookeeper Mack picks up one of the empty tortoise eggs and passes it to Maggie. "Do you notice anything special about this egg?" he asks her.

"The shell feels like rubber!" Maggie says, surprised.

"Many reptiles hatch from eggs that have soft shells," Mack says. "Speaking of eggs, I think you'd like to see some chicks over there."

The bird moms are very busy with their chicks. The ostriches, peacocks, and flamingos all have brand-new babies! Sonya Lee admires the flamingo's newborn chick and notices a crack opening in a second egg.

"Everyone, come here!" she shouts. "This egg is hatching!"

Just then, a little gray chick pops out of the egg.
"Why won't it open its eyes?" asks Sarah Lynn.
"It will," assures Zookeeper Mack. "All baby birds are born with their eyes closed. In a few days they will open."

"Aren't the zoo babies amazing?" Maggie asks Sonya Lee.

'Yes, but I wish there were lion cubs to see," she answers. "They remind me of my kitty at home."

The girls felt a gentle splash and realized that they were passing the dolphin pool.

"I think she wants us to notice her baby," laughs Maggie.

Zookeeper Mack laughs, too. "Dolphin mothers take very good care of their babies—often for several years. She seems very proud of her calf, doesn't she?"

Nearby, a walrus snuggles her pup close. "We see your baby, too," says Sonya. "He's adorable!"

The penguin habitat is always a busy place.

"There are so many chicks, it's hard to count them!" exclaims Eddie.

"I see lots of chicks, but no nests," Michael adds.

"Their nests are everywhere," says Mack. "You might not notice them because they are made of stones—not sticks and grass like other birds."

"Oooh, I see now," says Eddie.
"Another interesting thing about penguins is that the mothers and fathers take turns sitting on the egg until it hatches," adds Mack.

"Our zoo baby tour is over," says Mack. "Does anyone have any questions?"

"Before we go, can we see the lions?" asks Sonya Lee. "Even if there are no babies, they are still my favorite."

"Of course," says Mack. "Let's head over to their den."

"Look at the lion's pretty mane," says Sonya. "I wonder where the lioness is."

Then the friends hear quiet mewing sounds coming from inside the den.

"My goodness," says Zookeeper Mack. "Sonya, you may see lion cubs after all!

As the friends watch, the lioness pads out of the den with not one, not two, not three, but four brand-new cubs!

"They are beautiful," sighs Sonya. "Thank you for showing us your babies, momma lion. And thank you, Zookeeper Mack, for showing us all the animals."

"Anytime, friends!" he answers. "Come again soon!"

Seek and Find Fun!
Can you find all these things inside the book? Look carefully!

butterfly

seagull

balloon

chameleon

baby ostrich

bird

Pretty Patterns
Find the animals in the book that have these patterns.